W9-AWT-713

Rutti

MY BROTHER
TRIES TO MAKE ME LAUGH

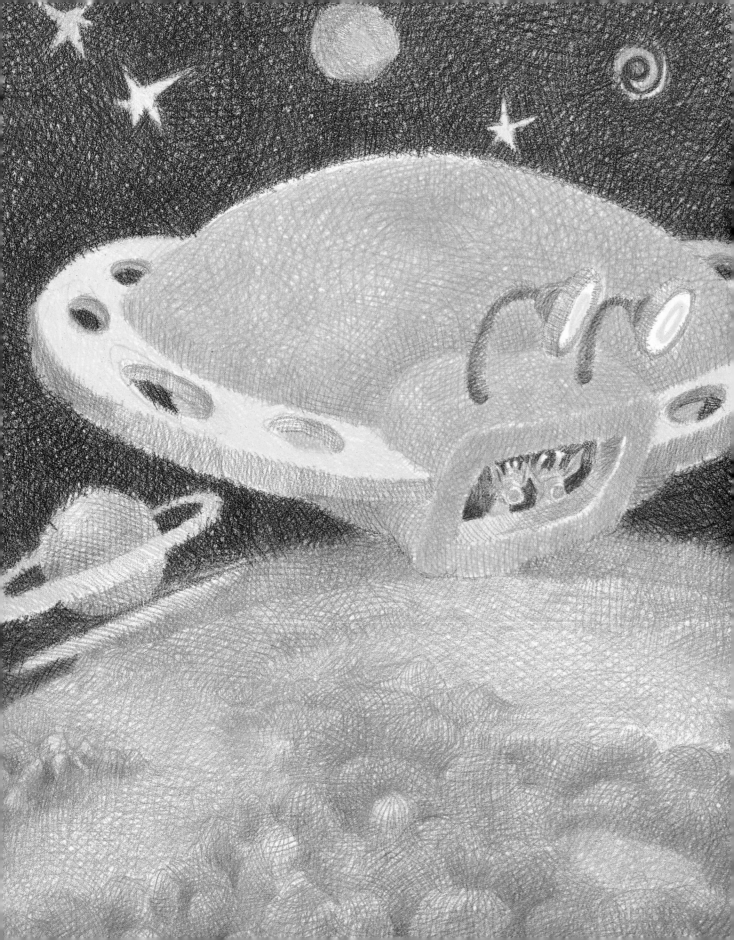

MY BROTHER
TRIES TO MAKE ME LAUGH

by Andrew Glass

Lothrop, Lee & Shepard Books   New York

Space Oddity words and music by David Bowie copyright © 1969 Westminster Music, Ltd., London, England. TRO-Essex Music International, Inc., New York, controls all publication rights for the U.S.A. and Canada. Used by permission.

Copyright © 1984 by Andrew Glass. All rights reserved. No part of this book may be reproduced or utilized in any form or by any means, electronic or mechanical, including photocopying, recording or by any information storage and retrieval system, without permission in writing from the Publisher. Inquiries should be addressed to Lothrop, Lee & Shepard Books, a division of William Morrow & Company, Inc., 105 Madison Avenue, New York, New York 10016. Printed in the United States of America. First Edition. 1 2 3 4 5 6 7 8 9 10

Library of Congress Cataloging in Publication Data. Glass, Andrew. My brother tries to make me laugh. Summary: Odeon tries to make his sister Zena laugh as they journey in a spaceship toward earth with their parents, Robot, and Computer. [1. Brothers and sisters—Fiction. 2. Science fiction] I. Title. PZ7.G48115My 1984   [E]   83-14989
ISBN 0-688-02257-X   ISBN 0-688-02259-6 (lib. bdg.)

Ground control to Major Tom

MY brother tries to make me laugh by making funny faces.

He jumps and hops and wiggles his fingers
behind his ears.

My brother cannot make me laugh by making
funny faces.

So my brother tries to make me laugh by telling silly stories. "All true," he says. "No lie."

"On Earth," says Odeon, "the children ride giraffes to school. They slide down their necks when school begins. When classes finally end, the children ride back home again."

At middle-time, Robot brings lunch.

My brother says, "On Earth, elephants live under tables and gobble up vegetables. They love lima beans especially. Elephants eat with their noses," he supposes.

He should know NOSES will never, never make
me laugh.

He says, "Every Earth family lives in a jumbo jet,
I'll bet.

"I feel certain that the elephants sleep inside, right under the tables. The giraffes, of course, are mostly at school all day with the children. Or they sleep standing up in the back yard. They rest their heads on treetops, I imagine."

Father laughs and rests his eyes. He lets Robot
drive awhile. My brother tries to make me laugh
all through the Milky Way.

After lunch, Mother drives. I wash the dishes and my brother dries.

Robot never does the dishes. He claims he isn't waterproof. Personally, I'm suspicious, because when we do our chores, he giggles.

When all the cups are vacuum-packed and all the plates suspended, Father calls, "Come over here, children, and take a look at this map. We are traveling to the third planet from the star that earthlings call the sun."

Father points ahead into space. "We will be landing soon, there, beyond the earthling moon."

"Computer," Odeon asks, "would you tell Zena why the earth's moon is covered with craters?"

Our machine squeaks and quickly speaks.

"Earthlings called Snackers come to the moon in rockets, carrying forks and shovels. They take home large moon rocks to eat—between meals—on salty crackers."

"No lie?" asks my brother.

"No lie," replies our computer, winking and blinking.

I'll bet Robot doesn't know how Odeon pro-
grammed Computer to tell stories of Snackers
and crackers and moons made of cheese.

But my brother will never, never, never make me
laugh with silly tricks like these.

"Please children, stop teasing the computer," says Mother. "And fasten those seat belts, both you and your brother. It's time to leave orbit. We're ready to land."

"Ask our giggly robot to lend me a hand as soon as he is off the phone," says Father. "We're about to become a U.F.O."

Our ship drops through the clouds and we circle the planet, over mountains and rivers and forests.

We zip past a crowded city next to an ocean,
and hover above a field of slanty-topped boxes.
"Look how neatly they grow," says my brother.

"Our earthling friends live in one of those boxes," says Father. "I see them now, in front of their house."

A mother earthling, a father earthling, a sister earthling, and a brother earthling are smiling and waving.

"Look at their tiny noses, Odeon, and such little ears!"

"I can't imagine how they hear," he says.

"It's true," says Mother sternly. "They do appear a little weird, but we don't want to hurt their feelings, so be friendly. Now that our landing has begun, let's see both of you smile, and no making fun."

"Welcome to our planet," says the earthling mom.

"We're glad you are staying at our house," says Andrew.

"In fact, we've prepared a snack for Odeon," says Dorothy. "Moon rocks and crackers."

"You mean you really eat that stuff? I thought I just made that up to make my sister laugh. But you don't really ride giraffes—do you?" my brother asks.

"Only to school," answers Andrew.

"And back again, of course," adds Dorothy.

The earthlings begin to giggle. They jump and hop and curl their fingers up behind their ears.

Then Dorothy asks Odeon, "Did you know your robot called ahead? It would make you laugh, he said, to offer moon rocks served with crackers, because you told Zena we were Snackers."

My parents laughed and laughed at that. The earthlings laughed along with them. Odeon laughed too, even though the joke was on him, and...

I laughed so hard I almost swallowed my nose.

"Earth is going to be fun," said Odeon.

"Like you," I said.